Jim Hunter books

Prisoner of
Pedro Cay

Ben Butterworth and Bill Stockdale
Illustrated by Maureen and Gordon Gray

Fearon Education
a division of
David S. Lake Publishers
Belmont, California

Titles in the Series

Jim and the Sun Goddess

Jim and the Dolphin

The Missing Aircraft

Jim in Training

The Sniper at Zimba

Prisoner of Pedro Cay

Danger in the Mountains

Race for Gold

The Diamond Smugglers

The Island of Helos

The Desert Chase

The Temple of Mantos

The Shipwreckers

The Killer Rocket

Sabotage in the Arctic

Rescue Mission

United States edition published 1980 by David S. Lake Publishers,
500 Harbor Boulevard, Belmont, California 94002. All rights
reserved. No part of this book may be reproduced by any means,
transmitted, or translated into a machine language without written
permission from the publisher.

First published 1977 by Methuen Educational
11 New Fetter Lane, London EC4P 4EE
Text © 1977 Ben Butterworth and Bill Stockdale
Illustrations © 1977 Maureen and Gordon Gray
Filmset in Photon Times 14 on 24 pt by
Richard Clay (The Chaucer Press) Ltd, Bungay, Suffolk
and printed in Great Britain by
Fletcher & Son Ltd, Norwich

ISBN-0-8224-3790-2

Printed in the United States of America

1. 9 8 7 6

Prisoner of Pedro Cay

'Well Jim,' said Colonel Johnson,

'how was your flying course?'

'Fine,' said Jim Hunter.

'I even did some hang gliding.'

'That's good,' said the Colonel.

'You may need a hang glider

for your next job.'

'What is my next job?' asked Jim.

'Art,' said the Colonel.

'Art,' said Jim.

'We don't know much about art.'

'Maybe we should,' said the Colonel.

'Look at this picture.

What do you think it is worth?'

'Don't ask me,' said Jim,

'but I painted pictures like that

when I was six!'

'It's worth a hundred thousand
dollars,' said the Colonel.
'That is – the real one is.
This is a fake.
Somebody stole the real one
and put the fake in its place.
Pictures worth millions
are missing all over the world.'

'What else do we know?' asked Jim.

'We have one fingerprint,'
said the Colonel.

'It was left on this fake.
The fingerprint of Harry Trent.'

'Harry Trent?' said Jim.

'He was a Bratt agent.
His body was fished out of the sea
somewhere in the West Indies.
Pedro Cay island, I think.'

'Right,' said the Colonel.

'It's a holiday in the sun
for you and Radar.

I want to know
who paints the fake pictures
and why Harry Trent died.

Jill will give you all the kit
and tell you about our contacts
on Pedro Cay.'

'What are these rubber dummies?'

asked Jim.

Jill laughed.

'Meet Tina and Leroy Gomes.

You may need their help.

You just blow them up

and dress them up

and you have two new agents.'

'I hope Radar won't bite them,'

laughed Jim.

'The real Tina and Leroy

will meet your plane,' Jill said.

'They are not real agents

but they are helping with this case.

Now, what about hang gliding kit?'

Jim looked down
at the clear blue sea
and the silver sand
as his plane came in to land.
No one was waiting for him
inside the airport.

He went outside.

There was no one there.

'Something must have gone wrong,'

Jim thought.

Then Radar's ears shot up.
'O.K. boy, find them, find them,'
Jim said.
He followed Radar
to a wooden hut
hidden among the trees.
Leroy and Tina were waiting there.
Leroy had been blowing
a dog whistle
pitched too high
for Jim to hear.

Jim laughed.

'I seem to have seen you two before,'
he said.

'We kept away from the airport,'
Tina said, 'in case we were
being watched.

Our boat is hidden
in the rocks.

Let's go before we are seen.'

They made their way to the boat
between the high rocks.
Leroy pointed to a small island
a short way out to sea.
'That's Pedro Cay,' he said.
'Harry Trent's body was found
washed up on the beach.
He had a knife in his back.'
They got into the boat
and headed for Pedro Cay.

'How well do you know
the island?' asked Jim.
'Like the back of my hand,'
replied Leroy.
'We have a small bar and shop
near the port.
Grandfather Gomes lives with us.
He drives the delivery truck.

We used to live with Father
in a cottage near the large house
on the island.
Father was an artist.
A stranger called Finster
bought the house and the cottage.
Just after that
Father disappeared.
The cottage is empty now.

They said Father had been drowned.
Some fishermen found his boat
smashed to bits on the beach.
But they never found his body.
Father was a good swimmer.
We think he is still alive
and Finster is keeping him prisoner.'

'Your father was an artist?'
said Jim.

'That fits.

We had better have a look
at this house.'

'Yes, Grandfather can take us in,'
said Tina.

'He delivers goods there.

Come up to the shop.

He is expecting us.'

'So this is the house,'
said Jim, looking hard
at the photo Tina gave him.
'It will be a job to get in.'
He could see that the house
was well guarded.
There was no way inside
except through the gates
and up a long drive.

'There's an armed guard
at the gate,' said Tina.
'Grandfather takes food
to the house in the truck
and we often go with him.
The guard checks us in
and checks us out.'
'I'm going in by hang glider,'
said Jim.
'You two are going in too,
but here's how you come out.'

They looked in surprise
as Jim inflated the rubber dummies.
'Grandfather takes you in,'
he went on.
'Hide in the cottage
and I will meet you there.
The dummies will take your place
in the truck on the way out.'

'It's too risky,'

said Grandfather Gomes.

'One man has been killed already.'

'It's the only way,' said Jim.

'I can radio the police

on the mainland

if we need more help.'

'O.K. we'll do it,'

said Grandfather Gomes,

'but wait until it's dark.'

When darkness came
Grandfather Gomes
drove up to the gate.
The guard looked inside the cab.
'Three of you and a dog,'
he said.
'You are very late.
Hurry up.'

Grandfather Gomes drove quickly
to the house and delivered the food.
As the truck left the house
Larry inflated the dummies.
The truck slowed up.
'Quick!' said Tina.

They ran into the cottage
with Radar and waited.
They heard the guard shout, 'Stop!'
as he peered out of his hut.
'One, two, three of you.
Where's the dog?'
There was silence.
'He's in the back, asleep,'
they heard Grandfather say.
'Right. Off you go,' said the guard.
It had been a tricky moment.
'That was close,' whispered Tina.

Jim had taken the hang glider
to the top of the cliff
above the house.
The wind was blowing steadily
in from the sea.
A good leap off the cliff
and Jim was away
dangling from the glider.
He rose up quickly
and came back over the house.
He dropped as silently
as a bird of prey
by the cottage.

Tina ran up to him.

'This way,' she whispered.

'Hide the glider in the bushes.'

Jim looked at Leroy.

'I saw Finster's boat
just below the cliff,' he said.

'Go down and fix it
while Tina shows me the house.'

Tina led Jim down into the cellar
and along a passage
which led to the house.
Then she put a finger to her lips.
'We are in the house now,'
she whispered.
Silently Tina slid open
a panel in the wall.

'Look, there's Finster,'
Tina whispered.
'And that's Bratt with him,'
Jim hissed.
They watched the two men
cross the hall to a statue.
Finster pushed its right eye.
The statue rose up on four pistons
to show a staircase below.
The two men disappeared
down the steps.

'Tina, you go back
to the cottage
and wait for Leroy,'
Jim said.
'I may need you both later.
I'm going after them.'
He slid back the panel
and followed the two men.
Radar followed close behind him.

He came to a large, well-lit room.

It was hung with stolen pictures.

At the far end of the room

Finster was talking to Bratt.

'This is Gomes,' he said.

'He paints my pictures.

You can hardly tell them

from the real ones

your men steal for me!'

Then Jim saw a tall thin man
chained to a metal table.
He had a picture in front of him.
'Now come and see my second room,'
Finster said.
Jim crept after the two men,
gun in hand.

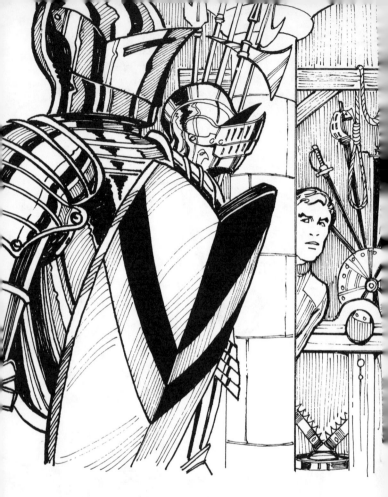

The second room was full of swords,
armour, gallows, a pillory
and even man-traps.
Jim hid behind a pillar.

Suddenly, his gun was knocked from
his hand and he was held tightly.
A suit of armour beside him
had come to life.
Radar barked,
and bit a leg of steel.
The suit of armour laughed.
'A lot of good that will do.
You never expected a guard
dressed up like this, did you?'

Bratt spun round.

'Jim Hunter,' he said,

white with anger.

'What does this mean?'

Finster asked.

'You fool!' shouted Bratt.

'It means that somebody knows

about this place

and about the paintings.

We had better get out of here fast.

Get the paintings on your boat.

I'll see to Hunter and Gomes.'

He pulled out a pistol.

'No,' said Finster.

'I hate guns.

I have a better way.

Bring Gomes in here,'

he said to the guard.

'Put Hunter in the pillory

and tie the dog up.

This room is under the sea.

They can all die together.'

He pulled a lever in the wall.

Sea water flooded into the room.

'We should have done this
to Harry Trent when he tried
to steal my paintings,'
said Finster.

Jim and Gomes watched the two men
disappear up the steps.

'There is still a chance, Mr Gomes,'
Jim said.

'Tina and Leroy are in the cottage.'

'But if we shout for help,
Finster and Bratt will guess
they are there,' said Mr Gomes.

Jim looked at Radar.

'Howl, boy, howl,' he said.

Radar lifted his nose

and set up a howl

that rang round the house.

They waited and waited.

The water was now rising
up to their waists
and only Radar's head showed.
Then suddenly he barked
as he heard footsteps.

A moment later

Tina and Leroy burst in.

'Father,' shouted Tina,

'I knew you were still alive.

I knew it!'

'Hurry!' said her father.

Larry grabbed a battle axe
from the wall
and smashed open the pillory.
Another blow with the axe
cracked the chain
holding his father.

Jim waded to Radar

and they all stumbled

up the steps.

The pictures on the walls had gone.

'Leroy, did you fix the boat?'

asked Jim.

Leroy nodded.

'I got the police

on your radio too,' he said.

'They should be just in time.'

Jim led the way
to the top of the cliff.
He looked round the bay.
'Police boats!' he shouted.
'They've got Finster
and the paintings!'

Then he looked up in the sky.

He watched a single seater plane

head out to sea.

'They didn't get Bratt,'

he said,

'but we shall meet again.'

'Well, Jim,

back from the world of art?'

said the Colonel.

'I've got something for you.

She's pretty too.'

'Good,' said Jim.

'What will it be –

a dinner or a dance?'

'Not for this one,'
laughed the Colonel,
holding up a painting
of the Mona Lisa.
'And you can't tell her
from the real one!'